THE CIRCUS of WORDS

ACROBATIC ANAGRAMS

PARADING PALINDROMES

Richard Lederer

WONDERFUL WORDS ON A WIRE

AND MORE LIVELY LETTER PLAY

Illustrated by
Dave Morice

CHICAGO
REVIEW
PRESS

Library of Congress Cataloging-in-Publication Data
Lederer, Richard, 1938–
The Circus of Words: acrobatic anagrams, parading palindromes, wonderful
words on a wire, and more lively letter play / written by Richard Lederer ;
illustrated by Dave Morice.
        p. cm.
Includes bibliographical references.
ISBN 1-55652-380-7
     1. Vocabulary—Juvenile literature. 2. Play on words—Juvenile literature.
3. Word games—Juvenile literature. [1. Word games. 2. Games] I. Morice,
Dave—ill. II. Title.

PE1449 .L335 2001
428.1—dc21   2001017471

To Kenya and her people

Cover and interior design: Sean O'Neill

Published by Chicago Review Press, Incorporated
814 North Franklin Street
Chicago, Illinois 60610
ISBN 1-55652-380-7
Printed in the United States of America
5 4 3 2 1

Contents

Order of Performances

AS WE ENTER THE GROUNDS OF
the Circus of Words, the barker calls us into the Big Top.

Circuses begin with music, and into the ring now rolls "The Bandwagon," in which the letter play must be heard to be fully appreciated. Among these sounds are those of letters themselves, one of the first things we learn about playing with words.

We are then treated to the two most famous acts of letter play—anagrams and palindromes in "Those Amazing Anagrams," "Ana Gram, the Juggler," "Palindromes on Parade," and "The Palindromedary." Palindromic words and statements can be thought of as a special kind of anagram. Letters are rearranged in anagrams, but in palindromes the rearrangement of letters in the second half of the word or statement can be only one way—backward.

"Clown Cars" introduces the idea of words hiding within words. In charade words, the larger words are composed entirely of smaller words, with nothing left over. The whole is the sum of its parts.

The next chapters extend the idea of words lurking within words. "The Shrinking Spotlight" shines upon beheadings and curtailments—larger words that become smaller words when certain letters are removed. "Kangaroo Words" are one especially lively member of this category. Letters are deleted from various locations in the parent words to produce joeys (baby kangaroos) that retain the original letter order and meaning.

Just as the previous chapters spotlighted the ability of words to become other words, "The Acro Bat" and "Silver Spoonerisms" show off letter clusters that fly through the air and change from one word to another—but now the creation of new words results not from deleting letters but from switching them.

"Words on a Wire" features words that tread narrow tightropes. The fun comes from the challenging restrictions placed upon the letters used to make new words. This is also the spirit of "Mary Had a Letter Lamb," which reviews many of the circus acts in this book through variations on one poetic theme.

"A Letter-Perfect Sideshow" exhibits an array of words beyond those already presented. This is an opportunity to show off some of the more bizarre words that dance through the entertaining English language.

The Barker

Dave Morice

Once upon a time, when the sky was made of canvas and the ground was made of sawdust, elephants in tutus danced on their toes and cradled showgirls in their trunks.

Once upon a time, fountains of red hair spouted from high white foreheads, and saggy, baggy clowns spilled into our laughter.

Dave Morice

Once upon a time, acrobats in spangled tights flew through the air like birds, and plumed horses pranced to the music of steam calliopes.

Once upon a time, there was magic in our land, and that magic was the circus.

Ladies and gentlemen! Boys and girls! Children of all ages! Hurry! Hurry! Hurry! Step right up and into a ring-a-ding circus of words! Inside, you'll ooh and aah at tremendous, stupendous, and end-over-endous words:

Words swinging from tent-tops!
Words teetering on tightropes!
Words swallowing swords and breathing fire!
Words leaping through flaming hoops!
Words leaping onto the backs of galloping ponies!
Words thrusting their heads into the jaws of lions!
Animal words—from Noah's aardvark to on beyond zebra!
High-caliber words shot out of the cannon of letter fun!

From land to sea, from A to Z,
You can bet the alphabet,
Like dancers on a spotlight stage,
Will leap and pirouette.

See dancing words, entrancing words,
Sterling words unfurling.
Watch prancing words, enhancing words,
Whirling, twirling, swirling.

You've played with letters a lot in your life. You may have told riddles and jokes like these:

- What word becomes shorter when you add two letters to it? *Short*.
- The difference between a *champ* and a *chump* is *u*.
- The dictionary is the only place where success comes before work.
- Why is the letter *D* like a naughty child? Because it makes *ma mad*.
- Why is *noon* like the letter A? Because it is in the middle of *day*.
- What starts with T, ends with T, and is full of T? A *teapot*.
- It occurs once in every minute, twice in every moment, and yet never in one hundred thousand years. What is it? The letter *m*.

and

- What is the longest word in the English language? *Smiles* because there's a *mile* between its first and last letters.

Your smile will indeed be a mile wide when you take your seat in the biggest top of all, the sawdust stage of words. Words are art. Words are entertainment. Words are a circus, where all the humor is guaranteed to be in tents!

The Bandwagon

LADIES AND GENTLEMEN!
Fit-as-a-fiddle boys and girls!
Noteworthy music lovers of all
ages! What you are about to see
will be music to your ears. As your
keynote ringmaster, I hope to strike
the right key and the correct note
in your love of letter play. So let's
hop on the bandwagon and face the
music!

Dave Morice

Now the tent grows dark, and the crowd grows hush.
Then the spotlight shines, and the space grows lush
With the cymbals' clash and the tinkled heat,
The triangle's ting and the snare drum's beat,
As our hungry hearts and the empty air
Fill to the brim with a brassy blare.

Our jaws a-droop and our eyes a-light
And our cheeks ablaze at the gorgeous sight:
All golden and crimson and purple and blue—
A calliope dream that we never knew:
With the chest-deep pulse of the kettle drums,
Into the ring the bandwagon comes.

Then the wha-wha-wha of the slide trombone,
And the pitter-boink-boink of the xylophone,
And the umpa umpa umpa umps
Of tubas kissed by men with mumps,
And the twang and the wang and the whacka whacka whack
Of banjo wheels on a circus track.

Ah, the rattle and rhyme of the music's time
Brim our hungry hearts with a song sublime!

Honored members of the audience! As I crack my whip, the
canvas castle fills with life. Onto the sawdust stage high-steps
our spectacular English language.

Dave Morice

Let's start with letter-perfect words. When you were very, very young, you may have sung this song:

> A sailor went to C-C-C,
> To see what he could C-C-C,
> But all that he could C-C-C
> Was the bottom of a great blue C-C-C.

This is an example of the similarity in sound between the letter *C*, and the words *sea* and *see*. Half the letters in the alphabet sound like words:

A:	a
B:	be, bee
C:	sea, see
G:	gee
I:	aye, eye, I
J:	jay
O:	oh
P:	pea
Q:	cue, queue
R:	are
T:	tea, tee
U:	ewe, you
Y:	why

When you pronounce some words, they consist entirely of letter sounds. Listen now to the effects (FX) of the most popular letter words:

any (NE)   escapee (SKP)
arty (RT)   essay (SA)
beady (BD)   excel (XL)
cagey (KG)   excellency (XLNC)
cutey (QT)   excess (XS)
decay (DK)   icy (IC)
easy (EZ)   ivy (IV)
empty (MT)   Kewpie (QP)
enemy (NME)   seedy (CD)
envy (NV)   teepee (TP)

Lewis Carroll, author of *Alice's Adventures in Wonderland* and other fantasies, played upon the sounds of letters in composing a letter to a young girl named Annie Rodgers:

My dear Annie,
I send you
A picture, which I hope will
B one that you will like to
C. If your Mamma should
D sire one like it, I could
E sily get her one.

A classic dialogue consits of the following string of letters that don't exactly match the sounds of words, but come pretty close. The scene is a restaurant, and the characters are a breakfast diner and a server. Say the letters aloud to hear the dialogue:

Diner (to server):   F U N E X?
Server: Y S V F X.
Diner: F U N E M?
Server: Y S V F M.
Diner: O K L F M N X.

The translation is:

Diner (to server):   Have you any eggs?
Server: Yes, we have eggs.
Diner: Have you any ham?
Server: Yes, we have ham.
Diner: OK, I'll have ham and eggs.

Don't you think that sounds pretty close?

If music be the food of love, play on! Play on we shall.

THREE-RING LETTER PLAY

1. Each of the following definitions yields a word that sounds just like a letter of the alphabet. Fill in each blank with the proper letter and then string the letters together to reveal the hidden message. Fill in the blanks you know with certainty first, and then figure out every variation for the remaining blanks. If all your answers are correct, you'll reap a rich reward.

_____ a honey of an insect; exist

_____ vision organ; pronoun

_____ exclamation

_____ a blue and white bird

_____ indefinite article

_____ large body of water; perceive

_____ woman's name

_____ green vegetable

_____ to be in debt; exclamation

_____ beverage; golf peg

2. Here's an example of letter play that appeared in the July 1903 *Woman's Home Companion*. ICQ out so that I can CU have fun translating the sound FX of this poem:

The farmer leads no EZ life.
The CD sows will rot;
And when at EV rests from strife,
His bones will AK lot.

In DD has to struggle hard
To EK living out;
If IC frosts do not retard
His crops, there'll BA drought.

The hired LP has to pay
Are awful AZ, too;
They CK rest when he's away,
Nor NE work will do.

Both NZ cannot make to meet,
And then for AD takes
Some boarders, who so RT eat,
And E no money makes.

Of little UC finds his life;
Sick in old AG lies;
The debts he OZ leaves his wife,
And then in PC dies.

3. Now hear the music of some letter-perfect verse. Keep in mind that the same letter twice in a row sounds like a plural. For example, II means "eyes."

YURYY
Is EZ to C
U should B called
"XLNC."

U XEd NE
MT TT.
I NV how U
XL with EE.

4. Open your ears to the sounds of the words that follow. What characteristic unites the words in each list?

1) seize, tease, use, wise

2) ate, for, to, won

3) bare, hoarse, new, towed

Answers

1. BIG JACKPOT

2. The farmer leads no easy life.
   The seed he sows will rot;
   And when at eve he rests from strife,
   His bones will ache a lot.

   Indeed he has to struggle hard
   To eke a living out;
   If icy frosts do not retard
   His crops, there'll be a drought.

   The hired help he has to pay
   Are awful lazy, too;
   They seek a rest when he's away,
   Nor any work will do.

   Both ends he cannot make to meet,
   And then for aid he takes
   Some boarders, who so hearty eat,
   And he no money makes.

   Of little use he finds his life;
   Sick in old age he lies;
   The debts he owes he leaves his wife,
   And then in peace he dies.

3. Why you are wise
   Is easy to see.
   You should be called
   "Excellency."

   You exceed any
   Empty tease.
   I envy how you
   Excel with ease.

4. 1) Each word sounds like the plural of a letter—c's, t's, u's, y's.
   2) Each word sounds like a number—8, 4, 2, 1.
   3) Each word sounds like the name of an animal—bear,
      horse, gnu, toad.

Those Amazing Anagrams

LADIES AND GENTLEMEN! Boys and girls! Welcome to the fabulous, sensational Circus of Words, the Greatest Show on Earth. Watch words come out of the wordwork. Gasp as letters fly through the air with the greatest of E's.

Can you create one word out of the letters in *new door?*

The answer is (ha ha) *one word.* The letters in *new door* are the same as those in *one word,* except in a different order.

When is enough not enough?

When you rearrange these letters you get only *one hug.* Everybody knows that one hug is never enough!

These riddles all involve anagrams. An *anagram* is a reordering of all the letters in a familiar word, phrase, or name to form another word, phrase, or name. The most high-flying anagrams use all the letters from the original word or phrase.

Feast your eyes on a parade of anagram crackers. Note that each italicized word is an anagram of the word that is its partner. Gaze with amazement as onto the circus stage trot a:

shore horse	*toga goat*
calm clam	*tan ant*
point pinto	*paroled leopard*

Are you ready to *greet* an *egret, count a toucan,* and recoil at a *snake sneak?*

Enter asp, in slithers *a serpent.*
Take a *gander;* stay outside the fence.
Ranged in the *Garden* of *Danger,*
A *serpent* at *present repents.*

Next in the parade march more animals where the letters in the first half of the description are rearranged in the second half:

lo, a girl gorilla	*any he hyena*
wee ewe	*one-sail sea lion*
trout tutor	*smug tan mustang*
orchestra carthorse	*cabaret bearcat*
taco cook cockatoo	*cop-outs octopus*
a steed seated	*grade B badger*
throne hornet	*leaf flea*

And there's more!

sobbing gibbons	*snug gnus*
spooled poodles	*slow owls*
noiseless lionesses	*the Nepal elephant*

For fun we'll close with *ten skit kittens* in a *cat act*.

Now watch now as certain words shuffle their letters and become other words that mean almost the same thing as the original word:

aboard/abroad	entirety/eternity
aloft/float	evil/vile
arise/raise	note/tone
aye/yea	it's/'tis
babbling/blabbing	rescues/secures
berrybush/shrubbery	statement/testament
brush/shrub	tired/tried
detour/routed	weird/wired

Dave Morice

Please give a big round of applause to the luminous, the bright, the twinkling star of our show. Boys and girls, I give you the word *star:*

Right off, you'll note *s-t-a-r* spells *rats* backward.

In fact, *star* is what is known as a perfect anagram, a word that can be rearranged into other words each beginning with a letter in the original word:

star	tars	arts	rats

Have you ever noticed that the STOP you see on signs yields six different four-letter words that begin with the four letters in STOP?

Our landlord *opts* to fill our *pots*
Until the *tops* flow over.
Tonight we *stop* upon this *spot,*
Tomorrow *post* for Dover.

That makes STOP a perfect anagram, too.

Last but far from least, there's the verb *eat.* Loop the *e* to the back, and you get *ate,* the past tense of *eat.* Now loop the *a* in ate to the back. After we *ate,* we washed the meal down with a cup of *tea.* The triple loop gives us another perfect anagram and forms three word squares:

EAT	ATE	TEA
ATE	TEA	EAT
TEA	EAT	ATE

THREE-RING LETTER PLAY

1. **By finding anagrams for the italicized words, can you solve this classic riddle?**

   In my front is a twisted *thorn*.
   On my right a scrambled *seat*.
   Behind me is a broken *shout*,
   And on my left is shattered *stew*.
   What am I?

2. **Rearrange all the letters in each word to make two or more other words:**

   mean
   now
   pool
   smile
   time
   tales

3. **In the poem below, fill in each blank with a word made from the letters *e, i, l,* and *v*.**

   A _____ old lady, on _____ bent,
   Put on her _____, and away she went.
   "_____, my son," she was heard to say,
   "What shall we do to _____ today?"

4. An anagram of *Richard Lederer,* the author of this book, is
    riddler reacher. Try constructing anagrams of your first and
    last names and those of your friends.

Answers

1. The italicized words are anagrams of *north*, *east*, *south*, and *west*. The answer then is "I am a compass."

2. *mean*: mane, name, amen
   now: own, won
   pool: loop, polo
   smile: slime, miles, limes
   time: mite, emit, item
   tales: steal, slate, stale, teals

3. A *vile* old lady, on *evil* bent,
   Put on her *veil*, and away she went.
   "*Levi*, my son," she was heard to say,
   "What shall we do to *live* today?"

Ana Gram, the Juggler

WE NOW PRESENT THE greatest juggler in the world, the very heart and soul of the Circus of Words—Ana Gram! She can twirl balls, clubs, plates, hoops, or flaming torches, but she's best when she's spinning letters. She starts with three letters, and when she really gets them going, she adds another and another and another and another, until the audience bursts into applause.

Dave Morice

Boys and girls! Children of all ages! Don't *waddle!* Don't *dawdle!* It's time for Anagramarama! Come and enjoy the fun *residing* at *ringside.* Once again, each italicized word is an anagram of the word or words that come before or after it.

I *enlist* you to be *silent* and *listen* to the *inlets* of my *tinsel* words. As we *begin* our *binge* of letter juggling, *please* don't even think about falling *asleep,* or your *retina* will not *retain* the anagrams that have for too long *continued unnoticed.*

Simple logic *impels* your positive *reactions* to Ana Gram's *creations.* Among *robust turbos,* she's a *dynamo,* even on a *Monday*—a *gagster* who will *stagger* you with her *latent talent.* She knows how to transpose a *sword* into *words,* which then *float aloft.* Each *snatch* of her *chants* will *reclaim* the *miracle* of language.

Ana Gram *loves* to *solve* your woes. She's a *singer* who *reigns* and will never *resign* as your *merriest rimester.* She's one of those *crowd-pleaser leapers* whose *dances ascend* to the *highest heights* as she performs a *toe dance* while relating an *anecdote.*

Ana Gram's *persistent prettiness* earns her *direct credit* for curing any *allergy* in the *gallery.* The *luster* of the *result* she'll unfailingly *rustle* up will produce an *elation* that you will experience down to your very *toenail,* a joy that will—from an *inch* above your *chin* the *fringes* of your *fingers*—*roost* in the *roots* of your *torso.*

She is the very *heart* of the *earth,* a *damsel* who merits *medals.* With a *lovely volley* of letters, she juggles a *cheap peach,* an *Argentine tangerine,* and *solemn lemons* and *melons.* At the same time she twirls *pastel plates* and balances a *maraschino* on her nose while playing two *harmonicas*.

Lucky ladies and gentlemen! *Cripes!* Just think of the *prices* we offer, as advertised in *English* on the *shingle* that hangs above our booth:

DISCOUNTER INTRODUCES REDUCTIONS

Look closely at the *poster,* and *presto!*—*boing! bingo!* What we have here is three ten-letter words, each a rearrangement of the other two!

Ana's performance is a *charm* that you see *march* before your eyes. After the *mite* of an *item* that follows, I guarantee that at no *time* will you *emit groans* from your *organs*:

Arty Idol

Watch Ana Gram, and you will see
Her act inspires *idolatry.*
Please do not come *o tardily,*
And *dilatory** please don't be.

*Adroitly*** Ana Gram will start
To alter *daily rot.* She's smart:
An *airy dolt,* an *oily dart*
She'll change into the *doily art.*

*dilatory means to be late
**adroitly means with skill or resourcefulness

Our Ana Gram is *an acrobat*—ACT ON A BAR—as she juggles letters *alphabetically* and laughs, "I PLAY ALL THE ABC."

Now for a GRAND FINALE—A FLARING END. You clearly have *the sense of humor* and think, *"Oh, there's some fun!"* So, for your entertainment, the Circus of Words presents a parade of words and phrases that anagram into other related phrases:

advertisements	I'm trade's events.
an aisle	is a lane
a chain smoker	I'm a hacker, son.
considerate	Care is noted.
conversation	voices rant on
a decimal point	I'm a dot in place.
dormitory	dirty room

Fourth of July	joyful fourth
gold and silver	grand old evils
Halley's Comet	shall yet come
monasteries	amen stories
old England	golden land
the postmaster general	He's letter post manager.
punster	Run, pest!
restaurant	Runs a treat.
revolution	love to ruin
saintliness	least in sins
signature	a true sign
snooze alarms	Alas, no more z's.
Southern California	hot sun, or life in a car
Statue of Liberty	built to stay free
the Supreme Court	Come trust up here.
tantrums	must rant
telegraph	great help
the tennis pro	He in net sport.
United States of America	An acute strife made it so.
Valentine poem	pen mate in love
Western Union	no wire unsent

No wonder that an anagram of *the anagram* is AH, AN ART GEM!

THREE-RING LETTER PLAY

1. In each of the following phrases, change the italicized word to an anagram of the other key word. In each case, the new word will be a synonym of the italicized word. Synonyms are words that mean the same thing.

   For example, in the phrase "*autographed* design," a synonym for the italicized word *autographed* is *signed*, and this is an anagram of *design*. Thus, you would change the first word to signed to produce "signed design."

   1) *remember* cellar _____
   2) *sees* section _____
   3) mother's *container* _____
   4) *complimented* diapers _____
   5) *oppose* sister _____
   6) married *fan* _____
   7) *hurry,* sleuth _____
   8) *gamester's* parsley _____
   9) entrap *father* _____
   10) generate *adolescent* _____
   11) sectional *shore* _____
   12) *hides* rubies _____
   13) *small* Batman _____
   14) *viewing* genies _____
   15) license *muteness* _____

Answers

1. 1) *recall* cellar
    2) *notices* section
    3) mother's *thermos*
    4) *praised* diapers
    5) *resist* sister
    6) married *admirer*
    7) *hustle*, sleuth
    8) *player's* parsley
    9) entrap *parent*
    10) generate *teenager*
    11) sectional *coastline*
    12) *buries* rubies
    13) *bantam* Batman
    14) *seeing* genies
    15) license *silence*

Palindromes on Parade

A PALINDROME IS A word, a *word row*, a sentence, or a longer statement that delivers the same message when its letters are read in reverse order. Take another look at the phrase *word row*, and you'll note that the message is the same both ways.

Palindromes make us shout. Here are some exclamations that are the same when read forward and backward:

Ah ha!
Hey, yeh!
Oh, ho!
Tut-tut!
Wow!
Yay!
Yo boy!
Ahem! It's time. Ha!
Har-har! Rah-rah!

Enter the Circus of Words with your very own palindromic family. There's *mom* (*a mama*) and *dad* (*a papa* or *pop*) and *sis* and *tot* and *pup*. And you may have brought along a few of your palindromic friends:

Ada	*Hannah*
Anna	*Lil*
Asa	*Mim*
Ava	*Nan*
Bob	*Otto*
Eve	*Viv*

The word *radar* was coined to describe a radio device used to locate an object by means of waves reflected from the object and received by the sending unit. The letters in *radar* form not only an acronym ("radio detecting and ranging"), but an especially happy palindrome for the two-way reflection of radio waves. Other five-letter palindrome words include:

DAD   TOT   MOM   SIS   PUP

Dave Morice

civic	madam	sagas
kayak	refer	sexes
level	rotor	solos

Now cast your gaze on the file of palindromic animals entering the sawdust circle. Read the description of each animal both forward and backward:

a mall llama	*a nut tuna*
dock cod	*bar crab*
tango gnat	*reedy deer*
Mars ram	*worm row*
star rats	*sleek eels*
tepee pet	*red nag gander*
sewer ewes	*snob big gibbons*
snore herons	*sad Napa Pandas*

After a *spider redips*, we'll *separate tar apes* and then *stack cats*, by placing a *taco cat* upon a base of *senile felines*.

We must turn to sentences to discover the most spectacular palindromes. Some people claim that the first sentence ever spoken was a palindrome. Adam to his amazement found Eve (who has the first palindromic name) by his side. Having no one to introduce him, he politely bowed and said: MADAM, I'M ADAM.

Name Me Man
● ● ● ● ● ● ● ● ● ● ● ● ● ●

Backward and forward, as you will perceive,
Read Adam's first greeting to dear Mother Eve:
MADAM, I'M ADAM. Now we can conceive
That her answer was simply: EVE, MAD ADAM, EVE.

Another famous palindrome describes the saga of George Goethals, who built the Panama Canal: A MAN! A PLAN! A CANAL! PANAMA!

Route Canal

• • • • • • • • • • •

There was a man who had a plan
To set a can inside a pan.
His critics tried to ban him, pan him. Ah!
A MAN! A PLAN! A CANAL! PANAMA!

Boys and girls! Word lovers of all ages! Now feast your eyes
on the best modern palindromic pyramid ever constructed:

A SANTA AT NASA.

SO MANY DYNAMOS.

NEVER ODD OR EVEN.

RACE FAST, SAFE CAR.

SPACE SUIT (I USE CAPS)

NIAGARA, O ROAR AGAIN.

NURSE, I SPY GYPSIES. RUN!

SIT ON A POTATO PAN, OTIS.

MAY A BANANA NAB A YAM?

ELK CITY, KANSAS, IS A SNAKY TICKLE.

DIANA SAW DR. AWKWARD WAS AN AID.

SIR, I DEMAND I AM A MAID NAMED IRIS.

RETTA HAS ADAMS AS MAD AS A HATTER.

MARGE, LET A MOODY BABY DOOM A TELEGRAM.

I SAW DESSERTS. I'D NO LEMONS; ALAS, NO MELON. DISTRESSED WAS I!

DOC, NOTE. I DISSENT. A FAST NEVER PREVENTS A FATNESS. I DIET ON COD.

No wonder that an anagram of *palindrome* is "*I modern pal.*" And no wonder that an anagram of *palindromes* is "*Splendor am I!*"

Dave Morice

THREE-RING LETTER PLAY

1. You aren't a *dud* if you ask *huh?* To learn more about palindromes, list as many three-letter palindromic words as you can.

2. Don't be a *boob* or a *kook.* List three four-letter palindromic words.

3. List as many words as you can—like *now, lap, pool,* and *stressed*—that spell a different word backward.

Answers

1. Examples include *bib, bob, did, dud, ere, eve, ewe, eye, gag, huh, mom, mum, nun, pep, pip, pop, pup,* and *tot.*

2. Examples include *deed, noon, peep, sees, ma'am,* and *toot.*

3. Examples include *pat/tap, pot/top, bats/stab, decal/laced, deliver/reviled, denim/mined, devil/lived, dog/god, drawer/reward, faced/decaf, gulp/plug, guns/snug, part/trap, stinker/reknits, straw/warts,* and *wolf/flow.*

The Palindromedary

LADIES AND GENTLEMEN!
We now present an exclusive interview with the Palindromedary —a two-headed push-me-pull-you camel that looks both ways and meets in the middle. Whenever the Palindromedary makes a statement, that sentence, SIDES REVERSED, IS the very same sentence. We're conducting this interview outside on the circus camel lot.

Dave Morice

Barker:	So you're the famous Palindromedary?
Palindromedary:	I, MALE, MACHO, OH, CAMEL AM I.
Barker:	I see that, despite your fame, you're wearing a name tag. Why?
Palindromedary:	GATEMAN SEES NAME. GARAGEMAN SEES NAME TAG.
Barker:	Is it true that you were discovered in the Nile region?
Palindromedary:	CAMEL IN NILE, MAC.
Barker:	How are you able to speak entirely in palindromes?
Palindromedary:	SPOT WORD ROW. TOPS!
Barker:	What kind of word row?
Palindromedary:	WORD ROW? YA, WOW! TWO-WAY WORD ROW.
Barker:	Let's talk about the Circus of Words animal acts. I heard that the trainer said an earful to the flying elephant in your menagerie. What was the trainer's command?
Palindromedary:	"DUMBO, LOB MUD."
Barker:	I hear Dan, the lion tamer, is sick in bed and won't get up.
Palindromedary:	POOR DAN IS IN A DROOP.
Barker:	So there won't be a lion performance today?
Palindromedary:	NO, SIT! CAT ACT IS ON.
Barker:	How come? Did Dan take some medicine?
Palindromedary:	LION OIL.

Barker:	Have you seen the big cats perform?
Palindromedary:	OH WHO WAS IT I SAW, OH WHO?
Barker:	Well, have you seen the big cats in action?
Palindromedary:	WAS IT A CAR OR A CAT I SAW?
Barker:	In addition to the big cat act, will we be witnessing performing dogs?
Palindromedary:	A DOG? A PANIC IN A PAGODA!
Barker:	I heard that somebody slipped something under one of the dogs.
Palindromedary:	GOD! A RED NUGGET! A FAT EGG UNDER A DOG!
Barker:	Why aren't the owls performing tonight?
Palindromedary:	TOO HOT TO HOOT.
Barker:	And the panda?
Palindromedary:	PANDA HAD NAP.
Barker:	And the elk?
Palindromedary:	ELK CACKLE.
Barker:	But where are the deer?
Palindromedary:	DEER FRISK, SIR, FREED.
Barker:	I understand that the menagerie also includes gnus and zebras.
Palindromedary:	O GNU, FAR BE ZEBRA FUN! GO!
Barker:	And did the gnus actually sing the *Star Spangled Banner?*
Palindromedary:	RISE, NUT! GNUS SUNG TUNE, SIR.
Barker:	Do the rats join them?
Palindromedary:	RATS GNASH TEETH, SANG STAR.

Barker:	What's one of your favorite human circus acts?
Palindromedary:	TRAPEZE PART.
Barker:	And what's especially exciting about the trapeze?
Palindromedary:	TEN ON TRAPEZE PART! NO NET!
Barker:	No net?
Palindromedary:	NO TENT NET ON.
Barker:	Shall we identify and summon the acrobats to perform with the trapeze artists?
Palindromedary:	TAB OR CALL ACROBAT.
Barker:	And how do the acrobats train children for their act?
Palindromedary:	PUPILS ROLL A BALL OR SLIP UP.
Barker:	Are there any acts that you would get rid of?
Palindromedary:	DUDE, NOT ONE DUD.
Barker:	Will the Circus of Words continue to get better?
Palindromedary:	ARE WE NOT DRAWN ONWARD, WE FEW, DRAWN ONWARD TO NEW ERA?
Barker:	Mr. Palindromedary, we thank you for such an entertaining two-way interview. Is it true that you are the only animal who can speak understandably in palindromes?

Palindromedary: YES, THAT'S TRUE. ALL OTHER ANIMALS SAY THINGS LIKE, "EKILS GNIH TYASS LAMINAR EHTOLLAE URTSTAHT SEY."

Dave Morice

THREE-RING LETTER PLAY

1. Complete each palindromic statement by continuing with the original letters backward. Sometimes you will just reverse the original letters. Other times, you will need to add a letter or leave off a letter and proceed backward. In the example REWARD MY . . ., you would add a G and then go backward to produce REWARD MY GYM DRAWER.

1) WON TON? . . . _____

2) LID OFF A . . . _____

3) RISE TO . . . _____

4) TOO BAD, I . . . _____

5) DRAW PUPIL'S . . . _____

6) STELLA WON . . . _____

7) EMIL ASLEEP . . . _____

8) RATS LIVE ON . . . _____

9) STAR COMEDY . . . _____

10) GO HANG A SALAMI . . . _____

2. Change each phrase below to a palindrome. To create each palindrome, change one or two words in each clue to a synonym.

    For example, starting with the clue "wooden crib," you would change *wooden* to *birch* and come up with the palindrome *birch crib*. Note how the *h* becomes the balancing letter in the middle of such a palindrome. Sometimes you'll need that extra balancing letter; sometimes you won't.

    1) angry dam _____

    2) speedy car _____

    3) my workout room _____

    4) canine god _____

    5) maritime van _____

    6) nosy offspring _____

    7) Nurses sprint _____

    8) mined Levi's _____

    9) Late? Drat! _____

    10) Bosses weep. _____

    11) straw skin blemishes _____

12) personal journal raid _____

13) bold toss _____

14) gave back diaper _____

15) snack containers _____

3. What's the longest palindromic phrase or sentence that you
    can make up?

Answers

1. 1) Won ton? Not now.
   2) Lid off a daffodil.
   3) Rise to vote, sir.
   4) Too bad. I hid a boot.
   5) Draw pupil's lip upward.
   6) Stella won no wallets.
   7) Emil asleep peels a lime.
   8) Rats live on no evil star.
   9) Star comedy by Democrats.
   10) Go hang a salami. I'm a lasagna hog.

2. 1) *mad* dam
   2) *race* car
   3) my *gym*
   4) *dog* god
   5) *navy* van
   6) nosy *son*
   7) Nurses *run.*
   8) mined *denim*
   9) *Tardy?* Drat!
   10) Bosses *sob.*
   11) straw *warts*
   12) *diary* raid
   13) bold *lob*
   14) *repaid* diaper
   15) snack *cans*

Clown Cars

INTO THE CIRCUS RING wobbles a small, many-colored car. The pint-size vehicle jerks to a stop. Doors open and out spill not one, not two, but up to a dozen bouncing, jouncing, pouncing clowns—clowns whose two lips are blue lips, whose tummies are pillowy, and whose trousers are billowy—saggy, baggy pants held up by giant safety pins.

Out tumbles a jumble of vagabond clowns in huge clumsy shoes; august clowns with high white faces; dwarf clowns in checkered coats; midget clowns in plaid jackets; broad-striped, polka-dotted, derby-hatted clowns on stilts; and straw-haired clowns, all bubble-nosed, great-eyed, buck-toothed, and flap-eared.

Around the ring scamper bucket-sloshing, custard-throwing, horn-tooting, pistol-squirting, plunger-pushing, bottom-kicking, nose-twisting, slap-sticking clowns—the funniest sight you've ever seen.

How can so many clowns fit into such a tiny vehicle? Some are midgets, and others have learned to fold their bodies so that they don't take up much room.

Charade words are like clown cars. A *charade word* is one in which the larger word can be divided into smaller parts that are themselves words. We'll start the charading by parading some animals that are made of two smaller words:

donkey	DON KEY
flamingo	FLAMING O
goat	GO AT
heron	HER ON
herring	HER RING
kitten	KIT TEN
parrot	PAR ROT
pinto	PIN TO
robin	ROB IN
sparrow	SPAR ROW
toad	TO AD

Dave Morice

A few circus creatures also join the charade by revealing animals within animals:

antelope	ANT ELOPE
meadowlark	ME AD OWL ARK
pigeon	PIG EON

Many other words divide themselves into fascinating segments. Don't let charade words *bewilder* you; just BE WILDER about how you look at them:

MUSTACHE !

MUST ACHE !

abundance	A BUN DANCE
attendance	AT TEN, DANCE
awesome	A WE SO ME
bowlegged	BOWL EGGED
discovery	DISCO VERY
impact	IMP, ACT!
important	I'M PORT ANT
legends	LEG ENDS
manicure	MAN, I CURE
mustache	MUST ACHE
office	OFF ICE
oftentimes	OF TEN TIMES
pleasure	PLEA SURE
pumpkin	PUMP KIN
puppet	PUP PET
sunglasses	SUNG LASSES
tapestry	TAPES TRY
weeknights	WEE KNIGHTS

Dave Morice

Many puns and riddles raid the concept of charades. Some retain the original spellings; some don't:

- When is a door not a door?
  When it's ajar (a jar).
- What's the cost of earrings for pirates?
  Two dollars. A buck an ear.
- I scream for ice cream.
- Triumph is simply *umph* added to *try.*
- In *The Circus of Words*, all the letter play is in tents.

Everyone loves a charade. The most magical charade words are those that yield other words that retain the original spelling exactly and are related to the original word:

- We *atone* to be AT ONE with the universe.
- We try to *avoid* A VOID in our lives.
- On a *beanstalk,* do the BEANS TALK?
- A *caravan* often includes A CAR, A VAN.
- A *conspiracy* is a CONS' PIRACY.
- A *cutlass* can CUT LASS and lad.
- A *daredevil* DARED EVIL.
- A *generation* is a GENE RATION.
- To be *gentlemanly* is to be GENTLE, yet MANLY.
- When you study *history,* you say, "HI, STORY!"
- If you *initiate* a trip to a restaurant, soon after you might exclaim, "IN IT I ATE!"
- An *island* IS LAND.
- A horseback rider will *reinforce* a horse's good habits by applying the proper REIN FORCE.
- A *soap opera* makes us sigh, "SO, A POP ERA."

1. Here are sixteen words, each three letters in length. Combine each word in the left-hand column with another in the right-hand column to make eight six-letter words. Each three-letter word must be used only once. Example: *tar* + *get* = *target*

bud	age
car	air
fat	den
gob	get
imp	her
man	ice
not	let
war	pet

2. Now the game becomes a little harder. This time, the three-letter words are simply listed in alphabetical order. For each of the twelve answers, you are to stitch together *any* two of the words below to make six six-letter words. Again, be sure that you don't use any item more than once:

ace	ore
ash	pal
car	per
end	rot
ham	sea
leg	son

3. Here's a challenging game. Discover the synonym for each clue word, and add the two clues together to form one eight-letter word that is a synonym for the word on the other side of the equal sign. For example, the clue *has to* + *hurt* = *facial hair* yields *mustache*; *has to* is a synonym for *must* and *ache* is a synonym for *hurt* and must + ache = mustache. Good luck!

1) slender + ruler = considering

2) light fog + oxidation = disbelief

3) chromosome + rank = produce

4) arrive + expires = funny acts

5) relaxation + precipitation = hold back

4. Collect five words of six or more letters that are made up entirely of smaller words.

Answers

1. *budget, carpet, father, goblet, impair, manage, notice, warden*

2. *ashore, carrot, hamper, legend, palace, season*

3. 1) *thinking*
    2) *mistrust*
    3) *generate*
    4) *comedies*
    5) *restrain*

The Shrinking Spotlight

MANY LOVERS OF CIRCUS life consider Emmett Kelly the greatest silent clown of all time. Kelly played Weary Willie, a hobo whose sorrowful expression never changed. Willie wore a tattered brown suit, large and leaky shoes, and the most raggedy derby.

In Kelly's most famous act, he would sweep up a spotlight. Trying to clean up the arena, Kelly would methodically set about sweeping the floor. Working his way to the middle of the stage, he would find a pool of light. Though it was obvious to the audience that the source was a distant spotlight, he tried to sweep the splash of brightness away.

As he swept from the outside inward, the ring of light grew smaller and smaller. Finally, it became but a dot that Kelly carefully whisked into a dustpan or under a canvas ground cloth.

Like Emmett Kelly, we can shrink words a little at a time. One way to reduce a word is by beheading it. We cut away its first letter, and still a word remains. The beheading of a word often produces a surprising result:

bone/one	*orange/range*
climb/limb	*slaughter/laughter*
close/lose	*there/here*
height/eight	*whose/hose*
hover/over	*women/omen/men*

Your stupendous, tremendous, end-over-endous Circus of Words now presents a poem about a seven-letter word that can be successively beheaded down to a single letter. (Note: A prelate is a high-ranking official of the church.)

The *prelate* did *relate* a tale
Meant to *elate* both you and me.
We stayed up *late* and *ate* our meal,
"*Te* Deum" sang in key of *E*.

Ladies and gentlemen! Boys and girls! Watch as we successively behead the six-letter word *pirate* until only a single letter remains:

PIRATE

⇓

IRATE

⇓

RATE

⇓

ATE

⇓

TE

⇓

E

Now comes the curtailments—words in which the last letter or letters may be removed and still remain words. Among the most fascinating curtailments are those that produce a new word that is quite different in meaning from the first word.

area/are   *needless/needles*
badger/badge   *possess/posses*
camel/came   *priest/pries*
first/firs   *quartz/quart*
heaven/heave   *rodeo/rode*
hiss/his   *weary/wear*

Dave Morice

Here is a curtailment riddle in verse. Can you supply the answer?

It's found in the sea like pirate's loot.
Cut off its tail, and now it's a fruit.
Cut off its tail once more and you read
The name of a vegetable small as a seed.

The answer is:

PEARL

⇓

PEAR

⇓

PEA

Our wordy circus is now proud to present a menagerie of hidden animals that run and swim and fly and crawl out of words when a single letter is removed. First, come beasts that emerge from single beheadings or curtailments. You're invited to *clamp* a *clam, crown* a *crow, feel* an *eel, rant* about an *ant, regret* an *egret,* and *share* a *hare.* Now discover a *puffing puffin, shrewd shrew, stern tern,* and other hidden animals:

beard/bear   *cram/ram*
been/bee   *drat/rat*
board/boar   *potter/otter*
boast/boas   *scat/cat*
cape/ape   *then/hen*

Dave Morice

Then march and romp animals that, with the vanishing of a single letter from the front or back, materialize from within *other* animals—a *boar* and a *boa*, a *beagle* and an *eagle*, a *fowl* and an *owl*, a *fox* and an *ox*, a *wasp* and an *asp*.

THREE-RING LETTER PLAY

1. Combining beheadings and curtailments can produce an interesting result. Supply the three words that are described in the following poem:

   > I am an odd figure.
   > Behead me: I'm even.
   > Curtail me: I'm twilight
   > And maiden in Eden.

2. By removing an initial letter, then a second initial letter, list the words that correspond to the following synonyms? The parenthesized numbers indicate the length of each base word. For example, the clue

   blackboard (5)
   tardy
   consumed
   yields *slate–late–ate*.

   1) rubbish (5)
      redness of skin
      left after a fire

2)   gulp down (7)
     slop around
     permit

3)   location (5)
     fabric
     highest card

4)   unchanging (6)
     furniture
     can do

5)   speak in church (6)
     grasp for
     every

6)   pulled (5)
     indebted
     married

7)   _____ in Wonderland (5)
     insects
     frozen water

8)   woman (5)
     first man
     what a beaver builds is

9) increasing (7)
    propelling a boat
    in debt
    part of a bird

10) play unfairly (5)
    warmth
    consume food
    location

3. Make up your own game of beheadings or curtailments.

Answers

1. *seven, even, eve*

2. 1) *trash, rash, ash*
   2) *swallow, wallow, allow*
   3) *place, lace,* ace
   4) *stable, table, able*
   5) *preach, reach, each*
   6) *towed, owed, wed*
   7) *Alice, lice, ice*
   8) *madam, Adam, dam, am*
   9) *growing, rowing, owing, wing*
   10) *cheat, heat, eat, at*

Kangaroo Words

LADIES AND GENTLEMEN!
Boys and Girls! Word lovers of all ages! Please turn your attention to the hippodrome track around the sawdust ring. Forget all the hype and hoopla, and fix your eyeballs on the greatest cavalcade of animals ever brought together!

Paraders of the Lost Aardvark

All the emperor's processions,
All his treasures and possessions,
Cannot rival half the pomp
Of animals that march and romp.

What soul among us does not thrill
To a fiery hoop and a lion's skill,
The chittering of a monkey's laugh,
The spotted grace of a slim giraffe?

Who can be deaf to the ponderous sound
Of elephants that shake the ground,
Leathery monarchs lifting high
Their trumpet trunks to canvas sky?

Who is so proud as not to feel
A secret awe before a seal
That keeps such slick and moist repose
Spinning a ball upon its nose?

Who can forget a mighty horse
Trotting through its circle course?
Who is so old who fails to heed
A lady in pink on a milk-white steed?

Boys and girls! Round and round the hippodrome track walk and run and trot and creep and fly and swim a tentful of animals that are hidden in the names of other animals. All you have to do is remove some letters from the animal word and a concealed animal will suddenly appear, with all the letters in its name preserved, in perfect order:

antelope/ape	*chicken/hen*
beaver/bear, bee	*hedgehog/dog*
chameleon/camel, hen	*mongoose/moose*
crocodile/cod	*rabbit/rat*
crow/cow	*weasel/eel*
dove/doe	*wolverines/wolves*

All of this beastly letter play serves to introduce the center of today's show. Prepare to be hopping glad as, at the end of the mighty menagerie, in bounds a troupe of cute-faced, tall-tailed, deep-pocketed, ab-original kangaroos.

Being a marsupial, a mother kangaroo carries her young in her pouch. *Kangaroo words* do the same thing: within their letters they conceal a smaller version of themselves. This smaller word is a joey, which is what a kangaroo's baby is called. The joey must be the same part of speech as the mother kangaroo, and its letters must appear in order.

The special challenge of kangaroo words is that the joey must be a synonym. It must have the same meaning as the fully grown word. In the poem that follows, the italics emphasize the kangaroo and joey words:

Ab-Original Words

Hop right up to those kangaroo words,
Slyly concealing whiz-bangaroo words:
Accurate synonyms, *cute* and *acute*,
Hidden *diminutive* words, so *minute*.

Lurking inside of *myself* you'll find *me*.
Just as inside of *himself* you'll find *he*.
Feel your mind *blossom*; feel your mind *bloom*:
Inside a *catacomb*'s buried a *tomb*.

Kangaroo words are *precocious* and *precious*
Flourishing, lush words that truly refresh us.
We're *nourished;* they *nurse, elevate* and *elate* us.
We're so *satisfied* when their synonyms *sate* us.

Kangaroo words both *astound* us and *stun*.
They're so darned *secure* that we're *sure* to have fun!
With *charisma* and *charm*, they're a letter-play wonder.
They *dazzle* and *daze* with their treasures, down under.

The letters of the joey must not be entirely touching. Like a
kangaroo, each joey word must take at least one hop through the
letters of the mother word. Although we find a *story* in *history*,
art in a *cartoon*, and a *cave* in a *cavern*, these are not true
kangaroos because all the letters in each joey are right next to
each other.

Dave Morice

Just when you thought the act was over, into the *arena area* bounds a troop of more kangaroo words! I guarantee that this final *burst* of ab-originality won't be a *bust*. I promise that this finale will prove not to be *superfluous*, but rather a *plus*. Indeed, these words will *dazzle* and *daze* you. In each pair, note how the joey is a synonym of the longer kangaroo.

Kangaroo Words	Joeys
allegiance	alliance
appropriate	apt
barren	bare
barricaded	barred
brush	bush
chocolate	cocoa
coldhearted	hard
contaminate	taint
disappointed	sad
discourteous	curt
entwined	tied
evacuate	vacate
exhausted	used
honorable	noble
knapsack	pack
lonely	only
masculine	male
playfulness	fun
precipitation	rain
rampage	rage

Kangaroo Words	Joeys
rotund	*round*
salvage	*save*
separated	*parted*
shadowy	*shady*
slithered	*slid*
splotch	*spot*
strives	*tries*
struggled	*tugged*
supervisor	*superior*
unsightly	*ugly*

Among the kangaroo words that yield the most *joviality* and *joy* are those that conceal multiple joeys. Open up a *container* and you get a *can* and a *tin*. When you have *feasted*, you *ate* and *fed*. Inside a *chariot* is a *car* and a *cart*. A *community* includes *county* and *city*.

Finally, at the end of the parade march a few kangaroos that conceal their own opposites, or antonyms, as they are called:

Dave Morice

81

Kangaroo Words	Joeys
avoid	*aid*
courteous	*curt*
encourage	*enrage*
feast	*fast*
friend	*fiend*
inattentive	*intent*
pest	*pet*
resist	*rest*
stray	*stay*
threat	*treat*
uh-huh	*uh-uh*

THREE-RING LETTER PLAY

1. Inside an *apple* you'll find an *ape*, with its letters in perfect order. And inside a *cranberry*, you'll find both a *crab* and a *crane*. List as many words as you can that have animals inside. Remember the animal name cannot have all its letters touching.

2. Identify the joey inside of each kangaroo word. The smaller word must be a synonym for the larger word:

joined	purged
latest	rampage
lighted	reclines
misdoings	uniformity
observes	wriggle

Answers

1. Examples include *believe/bee, brat/bat, blizzard/lizard, botany/boa, bottler/otter, brushing/bruin, caramel/camel, cart/cat, claim/clam, debater/deer, gloat/goat, grander/gander, heroine/heron, hoping/hog, hyphenate/hyena, lotion/lion, mackinaw/macaw, patting/pig, rectangle/eagle, smolder/mole, snacked/snake, steal/seal, steamed/steed, swarming/swan, throbbing/robin, towel/owl,* and *trigger/tiger*

2. *one, last, lit, sins, sees, pure, rage, lies, unity, wiggle*

The Acro Bat

THE FLYING TRAPEZE WAS invented in 1859 by a Frenchman named Jules Leotard. But the flying trapeze doesn't fly—acrobats do.

The catcher on the shorter trapeze kicks hard and lets his body slip down until his legs wrap around the trapeze. He reaches out his arms.

Across the Big Top, up on a high platform, the other flyers watch the catcher's rhythms closely. At exactly the right moment, one flyer grasps the trapeze, jumps up high, and swings out hard—beyond the realm of ordinary lives.

The drum rolls.

On the second swing out, the trapeze artist lets go of the bar and catapults high into the air, end over end. For one thrilling moment he soars to the very top of the tent. At the last second, the airy athlete reaches out and locks perfectly in the waiting grasp of the catcher.

Thrill-seeking children of all ages! High above the sawdust stage you are about to gaze upon words that fly through the air and change from one form to another along the way. Absolutely no flash photography, please!

Let's watch as one Circus of Words animal transforms itself into another and another, and still another, and then performs the trick all over again. This rhyme provides all the clues you need:

I fly like a baseball, a wing'd heavy hitter.
Change my first letter; I'm the pick of the litter.
Do it again; I'm a rodent—no flattery.
Now change my last, and you'll charge me with battery.

The bestial solution is: *bat/cat/rat/ram*.

I start as an insect. Now change my first letter.
Now I'm a rodent. Please make me one better.
Now change my middle. I'm a mighty woodlander.
Now change my first and then take a gander.

The animals in that poem are: *louse/mouse/moose/goose.*

A bat and a louse and a moose are not the only animals that can be transformed into other animals by the substitution of a first letter:

beaver/weaver   *guppy/puppy*
dog/hog   *hare/mare*
donkey/monkey   *seal/teal*

And a rat and a mouse are not the only animals that become other animals with the change of a middle or last letter:

bear/boar   *foal/fowl*
cod/cow   *lion/loon/coon/coot/colt*

Now that you're familiar with the fun of substituting letters, let's look at some word records.

Two two-letter words can generate a dozen new words when one letter is added at the start. The first one is *at*, which becomes *bat, cat, eat, fat, hat, mat, oat, pat, rat, sat, tat,* and *vat* when just one letter is added. The second word is *ad*. Add one letter and you get *bad, cad, dad, fad, gad, had, lad, mad, pad, quad* (counting *qu-* as a single unit), *sad, tad,* and *wad.*

The only four-letter word that can yield thirteen new words by adding a letter at the front (if we count *qu-* as a single unit) is *ills*. Have fun with another lucky thirteen when the addition of one letter transforms this word into *bills, dills, fills, gills, hills, kills, mills, pills, quills, rills, sills, tills,* and *wills.*

Ears generates twelve new words by adding an initial letter—*bears, dears, fears, gears, hears, nears, pears, rears, sears, tears, wears,* and *years.*

For a dozen variations on a six-letter word, look to *ailing* (again counting *qu-* as a single unit) and get *bailing, failing, hailing, jailing, mailing, nailing, pailing, quailing, railing, sailing, tailing,* and *wailing.*

Circus-word lovers enjoy changing one word into another by substituting just the vowel. Here's what you get with this nifty trick:

> A *flea* and a *fly* in a *flue*
> Were imprisoned, so what could they do?
> Said the *flea*, "Let us *fly*."
> Said the *fly*, "Let us *flee*."
> So they *flew* through a *flaw* in the *flue*.

This compact limerick about the flea and the fly suggests a challenge: How many one-syllable words can we turn into other words by inserting each of the five major vowels?

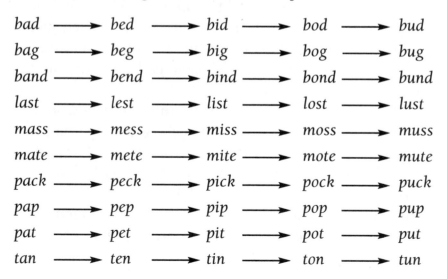

bad ⟶ *bed* ⟶ *bid* ⟶ *bod* ⟶ *bud*

bag ⟶ *beg* ⟶ *big* ⟶ *bog* ⟶ *bug*

band ⟶ *bend* ⟶ *bind* ⟶ *bond* ⟶ *bund*

last ⟶ *lest* ⟶ *list* ⟶ *lost* ⟶ *lust*

mass ⟶ *mess* ⟶ *miss* ⟶ *moss* ⟶ *muss*

mate ⟶ *mete* ⟶ *mite* ⟶ *mote* ⟶ *mute*

pack ⟶ *peck* ⟶ *pick* ⟶ *pock* ⟶ *puck*

pap ⟶ *pep* ⟶ *pip* ⟶ *pop* ⟶ *pup*

pat ⟶ *pet* ⟶ *pit* ⟶ *pot* ⟶ *put*

tan ⟶ *ten* ⟶ *tin* ⟶ *ton* ⟶ *tun*

Now we'll move up a syllable and listen to the jangle of a nursery jingle:

Betty Botter bought some butter,
"But," she said, "the butter's bitter.
If I put it in my batter,
It will make my batter bitter.
But a bit of better butter
Is sure to make my batter better."

So she bought a bit of butter
Better than her bitter butter.
Then she put it in her batter,
And the batter was not bitter.
So 'twas better Betty Botter
Bought a bit of better butter.

Dave Morice

Botter, of course, is not a word, but the rhyme suggests the challenge of finding a two-syllable pattern that can integrate all five major vowels, one at a time. Four sequences fill the bill:

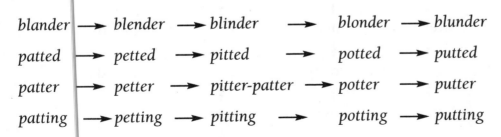

blander ⟶ blender ⟶ blinder ⟶ blonder ⟶ blunder

patted ⟶ petted ⟶ pitted ⟶ potted ⟶ putted

patter ⟶ petter ⟶ pitter-patter ⟶ potter ⟶ putter

patting ⟶ petting ⟶ pitting ⟶ potting ⟶ putting

It's even more fun to change every letter of a word to create another word. The star of our word-into-word show is the ac-ro-nimble, par-a-no-mazing Acro Bat. Watch now as the daring young bat on the flying trapeze ascends the word ladder on the way to its breath-defying performance.

Lewis Carroll, the author of *Alice in Wonderland* and other fantasies for children, invented a game called word ladders. The object is to change one letter at each step, while keeping the other letters in the same order. The goal is to change the first word into another word, often the opposite of the original.

Gape as the Acro Bat ascends the ladder, begins with one word, and ends up at the opposite or contrasting word:

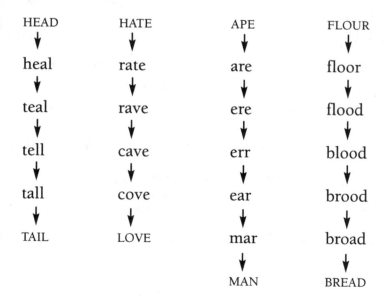

HEAD	HATE	APE	FLOUR
heal	rate	are	floor
teal	rave	ere	flood
tell	cave	err	blood
tall	cove	ear	brood
TAIL	LOVE	mar	broad
		MAN	BREAD

Dave Morice

THREE-RING LETTER PLAY

Transform the first word into the second word by changing one letter at a time in the number of steps indicated by the parenthesized number. In CAT to DOG (3), the sequence could be CAT–COT–COG–DOG or CAT–COT–DOT–DOG.

1) SAND to ROCK (4)

2) TRY to WIN (4)

3) HEAT to COLD (4)

4) LESS to MORE (4)

5) LEAD to GOLD (3)

Answers

1) SAND–SANK–RANK–RACK–ROCK

2) TRY–TOY–TON–TIN–WIN

3) HEAT–HEAD–HELD–HOLD–COLD

4) LESS–LOSS–LOSE–LORE–MORE

5) LEAD–LOAD–GOAD–GOLD

10
Silver Spoonerisms

LADIES AND GENTLEMEN!
Boys and girls! For our closing act
of soaring from word to word we
shall gag you with a spoonerism!

Near London in 1844 the
Reverend William Archibald
Spooner was born with a silver
spoonerism in his mouth.

He tended to reverse letters and syllables to produce many tips of the slung. For example, he once supposedly lifted his glass in honor of Queen Victoria. As he toasted the reigning monarch, he exclaimed, "Three cheers for our queer old dean!"

Dr. Spooner was a distinguished dean at Oxford University. He was so famous for his frequent tips of the slung that these switcheroos have become known as *spoonerisms*.

Ladies and gentlemen! Gadies and lentlemen! In honor of Dr. William Archibald Spooner's tang-tongueled whiz and witdom, we present a parade of spoonerized circus animals. See if you can pick out all the reversals in the following poem:

Dr. Spooner's Animal Act

Welcome, ladies; welcome gents.
Here's an act that's so in tents:
An absolute sure-fire parade,
A positive pure-fire charade—
With animals weak and animals mild,
Creatures meek and creatures wild,
With animals all in a row.
We hope that you enjoy the show.

Gallops forth a curried horse,
Trotting through a hurried course.
Ridden by a loving shepherd
Trying to tame a shoving leopard.

Don't think I'm a punny phony,
But next in line's a funny pony.
On its back a leaping wizard,
Dancing with a weeping lizard.

Watch how that same speeding rider
Holds aloft a reading spider.
Now you see a butterfly
Bright and nimbly flutter by,
Followed by a dragonfly,
As it drains its flagon dry.
Step right up; see this mere bug
Drain the drink from his beer mug.

Lumbers forth a honey bear,
Fur as soft as bunny hair.
Gaze upon that churning bear,
Standing on a burning chair,
Gently patting a mute kitten,
On each paw a small cute mitten.
Watch as that small, running cat
Pounces on a cunning rat.

See a clever, heeding rabbit
Who's acquired a reading habit,
Sitting on his money bags,
Reading many bunny mags,

Which tickle hard his funny bone,
As he talks on his bunny phone.
He is such a funny beast,
Gobbling down his bunny feast.

Dave Morice

Gasp in awe as winking seals
Sit atop three sinking wheels.
Don't vacillate. An ocelot
Will oscillate a vase a lot.
There's a clever dangling monkey
And a stubborn, mangling donkey
And—a gift from our Dame Luck—
There waddles in a large lame duck.

Dave Morice

That's Dr. Spooner's circus show.
With animals all in a row,
(As you can see, we give free reign
To this metrical refrain.)
Now hops a dilly of a frog
Followed by a frilly dog.
Hear that hoppy frog advise:
"Time's fun when you're having flies!"

THREE-RING LETTER PLAY

1. What's the difference between a church bell and a thief? One peals from the steeple while the other steals from the people. Fill in each blank below to complete each spoonerized expression:

   1) Chilly lasses are cold _____.
      Blonde ringlets are _____ _____.

   2) Rotten lettuce makes a bad _____.
      A depressing song is a _____ _____.

   3) A large needle is a big _____.
      Hogs eat out of a _____ _____.

   4) Dark bulls and cows are brown _____.
      A war for the throne is a _____ _____.

   5) A fisherman baits his _____.
      A lazy schoolboy _____ his _____.

2. Finish the set-up story by completing the spoonerized *pun*chline:

   An ancient jungle king tyrannized his subjects and forced them to build one elaborate throne after another. First, they constructed a throne of mud, then bamboo, then tin, then copper, then silver, and so on. When the monarch grew tired of each throne, he would store it in the attic of his grass hut. One day the attic collapsed, and the thrones crashed down upon the chief's head and killed him.

The moral of the tale is: "People who live in grass houses shouldn't _____ _____."

3. Spoonerize the first and last names of members of your class or family and see if you come up with something funny.

Answers

1. 1) cold girls/gold curls
    2) bad salad/sad ballad
    3) big pin/pig bin
    4) brown cattle/crown battle
    5) baits his hooks/hates his books

2. "People who live in grass houses shouldn't stow thrones."

Words on a Wire

WAY UP HIGH, AT THE very top of the Big Top, more than a hundred feet above the ring, a metal cable less than an inch wide stretches between two tall towers. This is the lofty world of the high-wire, or tightrope walker.

Dave Morice

Onto the dangerously swaying rope ventures the wire walker—a miracle of balance, in defiance of danger. High above the crowd, the walker dances across the airy stretch and treads on space. The band plays a slow waltz, then the drum rolls while thousands of eyes watch.

Some tightrope walkers hold a long pole to help them balance. Some even ride a bike. Our wire-walking words use nothing but the beauty and economy of their forms as they dance and even jump rope along a bridge of thread in the air high above the crowd.

First onto the wire is a cluster of one-syllable words that— believe it or not, and you soon will believe it!—do not include any of the major vowels, *a, e, i, o,* or *u!* That's right, ladies and gentlemen and boys and girls. You won't find any *ladies* or *gentlemen* or *boys* or *girls* in these words.

Among words that lack the major vowels are *by, cry, cyst(s), dry, fly, fry, gym(s), gyp(s), hymn(s), lymph, lynch, lynx, my, nymph(s), ply, pry, shy, sky, sly, spry, spy, sty, synch, thy, try, why,* and *wry.*

Add two letters to *cry,* and you get *crypt.**

Add two letters to *try,* and still avoid using any major vowels in *tryst.***

Add two letters to *my,* and you get *myth;* add three and you get *myrrh.****

---

* a chamber wholly or partly underground
** an agreement to meet
*** a yellowish brown to reddish brown aromatic gum resin with a bitter, slightly pungent taste, obtained from a tree

Among two-syllable words that exclude *a, e, i, o,* and *u* are *gypsy, pygmy, flyby,* and the abverbs *dryly, shyly, slyly, spryly,* and *wryly.* Each of these possesses two *y*'s, but one common two-syllable word of this type includes only one *y.*

The word is *rhythm(s).*

One three-syllable word also avoids the major vowels. This word is *syzygy,* which *Merriam Webster's Collegiate Dictionary* defines as "the nearly straight-line configuration of three celestial bodies in a gravitational system (such as the sun, moon, and earth)." *Syzygy* is an especially appropriate spelling for such a heavenly three-syllable word.

Once did a *shy* but *spry gypsy*
Spy a *pygmy,* who made him feel tipsy.
Her form, like a *lynx, sylph,* and *nymph,*
Made all his *dry* glands feel quite *lymph.*

He felt so in *synch* with her *rhythm*
That he hoped she'd *fly* to the *sky* with him.
No *sly myth* would he *try* on her;
Preferring to *ply* her with *myrrh.*

When apart, he would *fry* and then *cry,*
Grow a *cyst* and a *sty* in his eye.
That's *why* they would *tryst* at the *gym,*
By a *crypt,* where he'd write a *wry hymn.*

Her he loved to the *nth* degree,
Like a heavenly *syzygy.*

Dave Morice

Now onto the tightrope venture mirror words. To reflect on what a mirror word is and capitalize on the tricks that they play in a looking glass, please hold the next line up to the nearest mirror:

A B C D E F G H I J K L M N O P Q R S T U V W X Y Z

The letters that possess vertical symmetry—meaning that their left and right sides are mirror images of each other—are *A, H, I, M, O, T, U, V, W, X,* and *Y.* These eleven letters individually appear the same in a mirror as they do on a page. In a sense, each letter is a self-contained palindrome.

Note how in the conversation between the two owls that follows, each letter contains left-right symmetry:

"TOO HOT TO HOOT!"
"TOO HOT TO WOO!"
"TOO WOT?"
"TOO HOT TO HOOT!"
"TO WOO!"
"TOO WOT?"
"TO HOOT! TOO HOT TO HOOT!"

Next marches in a take-off on Henry Wadsworth Longfellow's "Hiawatha." In "AHTAWAIH," each character is letter-perfect but word-crazy. To get to the shores of Gitchie Gumee, you'll need to hold the poem up to the mirror:

OTTO TUOHTIW OTUA TAHT HTIW
IIAWAH TA AHTAWAIH
—!IXAT A TAHW—IXAT A TIH
.IMAIM TA ATOYOT A

.YVI OT WOV I TUH A TA
.IXAT A TIH AHTAWAIH"
HATU OT TUO TI WOT YAM I
"!YXAW OOT—WOT OT TIAW YAM I

IXAT A HTIW OTTO TUOHTIW
IIAWAH TA AHTAWAIH
-IXAM A—AMIXAM A TIH
!IMAIM TA (OTUA YM) AM

:AVA HTIW TUH A TA MA I
.OTUA YM TIH AHTAWAIH"
.ITIHAT OT TI WOT YAM I
".OTTO OT TOOT OT TIAW YAM I

AHTAWAIH HTIW YOT YAM I
.OIHO—AWOI TA TUO
IXAT HTOMMAM TAHT WOT YAM I
.UHAO OT—IIAWAH OT

Next out onto the almost-invisible high wire are the flying pangrams. Many typists know *The quick brown fox jumps over a lazy dog* as a 33-letter sentence that employs every letter in the alphabet at least once. Such sentences are called *pangrams*.

Look up at the canvas heavens and fix your eyes on a sampling of the best pangrams of even fewer letters. What you are about to see are meaningful sentences that avoid obscure words yet contain every letter of the alphabet:

Pack my box with five dozen liquor jugs. (32 letters)
Jackdaws love my big sphinx of quartz. (31)
How quickly daft jumping zebras vex. (30)
Quick wafting zephyrs vex bold Jim. (29)
Waltz, nymph, for quick jigs vex Bud. (28)
Bawds jog, flick quartz, vex nymph. (27)

And now, ladies and gentlemen, the Peter Pangram of all pangrams—

Mr. Jock, TV quiz Ph.D., bags few lynx. (26!)

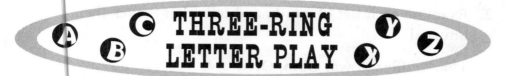

THREE-RING LETTER PLAY

1. This circus act has been about words with a very limited number or category of letters. In each list that follows, a parade of letters marches in alphabetical order. What do the letters in each line have in common? In this first section, try to discover what design element accounts for the unity.

   1) AEFHIKLMNTVWXYZ

   2) abcdefghjmnopqrstu

   3) BCDEHIKOX

   4) HINOSXZ

   5) ABDOPQR

   What concept other than shape unites each of the following groupings of letters?

   6) AEIOU

   7) AJKQ

   8) ABCGIJOPQRTUY

   9) CDILMVX

   10) ABCDEFGHIJKLMNOPRSTUVWXY

2. Examine each list of words and tell what makes them unusual.

1) area, idea, Iowa, Ohio, Oreo

2) baggage, cabbage, defaced

3) civic, livid, mimic, vivid

4) audio, eerie

5) loll, lull, sass

Answers

1. 1) All the letters are made with straight lines.
   2) All the letters are made with curved lines.
   3) All letters have horizontal symmetry.
   4) These letters remain the same when turned upside down.
   5) These letters contain enclosed spaces.
   6) These are the vowels.
   7) These are the letters on playing cards.
   8) These letters sound the same as a full word: *a, bee, see/sea, gee, eye/I/aye, jay, o/oh, pea/pee, cue/queue, are, tea/tee, you/ewe/yew, why.*
   9) These are Roman numerals.
   10) These letters are on a telephone dial, which lacks a *q* and *z*.

2. 1) Each word has three syllables but only four letters.
   2) These are called piano words because they are spelled entirely with the letters that span A through G, the notes on the musical scale.
   3) These are Roman numeral words, and *civic* is a Roman numeral palindrome.
   4) Here we have two five-letter words with just a single consonant.
   5) Three-quarters of each word consists of a single consonant.

Mary Had a Letter Lamb

LADIES AND GENTLEMEN! Children from eight to eighty! Lasses in Wonderland! Wizard of Ahs! Hurry, hurry, hurry!

Step right out and step right up! Beyond the Big Top you'll find the concession stands, where you can:

Feast your eyes and gorge your ears and lick
Your lips at apple words perched on a stick—
Popped-buttery words, words like roasted peanuts,
Words to fill up all you A-B-C nuts.

Syrupy, fizzy words! Don't walk, please run,
For steaming hot-dog words, snug in a bun;
Chocolate-covered words; and pink words spun
Sweet as cotton candy. Oh, what fun!

Dave Morice

After the food booths, you come to the petting zoo, with its cuddly calves, goats, and deer. There crowds flock and flocks crowd to see one of the star attractions of the circus—Mary's letter lamb.

Perhaps the most famous of all poems for little boys and girls is the eight lines of verse composed by Sarah Josepha Hale and published in 1830 in *Poems for Our Children:*

Mary had a little lamb,
Its fleece was white as snow,
And everywhere that Mary went
The lamb was sure to go;

Dave Morice

He followed her to school one day,
That was against the rule;
It made the children laugh and play
To see a lamb in school.

Dave Morice

We wonder if Ms. Hale would hail the things that happen to
her letter lamb when letter players play with her lambie. In each

of the versions that you are about to view, the poet uses a wild and wooly form of letter recreation to rewrite Hale's creation.

Let's start with an *acrostic* in which the first letters of the first stanza spell MARY and the first letters of the second row spell LAMB:

Mary had a little lamb,
A ram with fleece like snow;
Reacting to where Mary went,
Young lamb was sure to go;

Lamb followed her to school one day,
A flouting of the rule;
Making children laugh and play,
Beholding lamb at school.

Now read our lipograms. A *lipogram* is a statement or poem from which a key letter has been left out. Here is a lipogrammatic version of "Mary Had a Little Lamb," with *e*, the most frequently used letter in the alphabet, omitted:

Mary had a tiny lamb,
Its wool was pallid as snow;
And any spot that Mary did walk
This lamb would always go.

This lamb did follow Mary to school,
Although against a law;
How girls and boys did laugh and play
That lamb in class all saw.

And without *a*:

Polly owned one little sheep,
Its fleece shown white, like snow;
Every region where Polly went
The sheep did surely go;

He followed her to school one morn
(Which broke the rigid rule);
The children frolicked in their room
To see the sheep in school.

Just as lipograms bar certain letters, the *univocalic* excludes all vowels but one. Here's Mary and her letter lamb with *e* as the only vowel:

Meg kept the wee sheep,
The sheep's fleece resembled sleet;
Then wherever Meg went
The sheep went there next;

He went where she heeded her texts,
The precedent he neglected;
The pre-teens felt deep cheer
When the sheep entered there.

In *Anguish Languish*, Howard L. Chace invented a method of double-sound punnery to narrate furry tells (fairy tales) and noisier rams (nursery rhymes). Using this loopy language, Chace replaced the words in the original versions with words that are similar but never quite the same in sound. Here the first stanza is Chace's, the second ours. Oriole ratty? Den less gat stuttered!

Marry hatter ladle limb.
Itch fleas worse widest snore;
An ever-wear debt Marry win
Door limb worse shorter gore.

High fallow dear tusk cool wand hay.
Thought wars aghast door who'll;
Id meade thatch hill drain lift and plea
Deuce he a limb ads cool.

Moving right along to anagrams, here's a version of Mary and her pet in which the two stanzas are anagrams of each other:

A girl once kept a tiny sheep,
Widely famed for whiteness;
This pet would dog her every step,
No certain sign of brightness.

'Twas viewed, the pest, one day in class
By impish children there;
Kids laugh to see pets, goofing off,
Weren't trying—open, err!

Now it's time for a palindromic Mary. Each line of the poem reads the same forward and backward:

Mary bred a Derby ram,
Won some gem o' snow.
Went one romp more, not new
O gods, Mary, rams do go!

Walks a ton, not ask law—
'Loof drag gal, laggard fool.
Mar damn mad ram
Loots Mary, ram, stool.

As a grand finale to the sensational, recreational fun with Mary and her letter lamb, let's play around with spoonerisms:

Larry lad a middle ham.
Flits niece was sight as woe.
And every there what wary meant,
The gam was lure to show.

He hollowed fur to school done way,
Watch whiz arraignst the ghoul.
Skit plaid the ildren chaff and may
Sue lee a scam at tool.

Ladies and gentlemen! I'm grateful that you have allowed me to pull your eyes over the wool. And with that pun, I'll take it on the lamb.

THREE-RING LETTER PLAY

Dave Morice, the illustrator of this book, offers three other forms of Mary's adventures. What kind of verbal play runs through each version below?

May's Lamb

Young May had a wee small lamb,
Its fleece was white as snow;
And to each place that young May went,
The lamb was sure to go.

It went with her to school one day,
That broke some sort of rule.
It made the kids all laugh and play
To see a lamb in school.

Mary's Lambkin

Mary purchased tiny lambkin
Snowlike fleeces covered.
Every pathway Mary traveled
Thereat lambkin hovered.

Lambkin followed Mary schoolward,
Countered legal ruling,
Making playful children chuckle
Seeing lambkin's schooling.

Marilyn's Lambikin

Marilyn's ownership! Minuscule lambikin
Maximized fleeciness snowily.
Certainly everywhere Marilyn visited Lambikin visited showily.

Yesterday lambikin, following Marilyn
Scholarly, misbehaved lawlessly.
Schoolfellows visualized laughingly, playfully,
Scholarly lambikin flawlessly.

Answers

All the words in the first poem have one syllable; in the second poem, two syllables; and in the third, three syllables.

A Letter-Perfect Sideshow

OUTSIDE THE BIG TOP stand the sideshows. There men and women and boys and girls of all ages strain to see the human skeleton who makes no bones about giving you the skinny; the iron-pumping strong man; the illustrated multimedia tattooed man; the snake charmer, who works for scales; the bearded lady, who always wins by a whisker by earning her bread with her bared beard; and the India rubber man, who bends over backward beyond any stretch of the imagination.

Dave Morice

Jest for the pun of it, audiences look up to the giant, whose positive altitude reaches new heights of entertainment; the dog-faced boy who performs in the pup tent and is studying to become a barker; the Egyptian princess of a thousand veils—always in a state of de Nile; the sword swallower, always on the cutting edge; the Siamese twins; the alligator man; the lobster boy; the mule-faced girl; the wild man of Borneo; and other exotic attractions bound to evoke your admission that they are more than worth the price of admission.

Ladies and gentlemen! Boys and girls! Step out of the main tent and tour an exhibition of the world's most spectacular words, those fantastic freaks of nature and confounding curiosities.

Ace

In *ace*, the first, third, and fifth letters of the alphabet are joined. Ho hum, you yawn, and I agree because I haven't been playing with a full deck. But think about this: If you add up the number of letters in a standard deck of cards—ace (equals three because it has three letters) + king + queen + jack + ten + nine + eight + seven + six + five + four + three + two—the total comes to 52, the total number of cards!

Arm

Arm is one of more-than-you-might-guess body parts spelled with just three letters. Lend your ear to and cast your eye on *ear, eye, gum, gut, hip, jaw, lap, leg, lid, lip, rib,* and *toe.*

Begins

A small community of six-letter words are composed of letters that appear in alphabetical order without repetition. Among them are *abhors, almost, begins, chimps,* and *chinos.*

Billowy

This is the longest word (seven letters) in alphabetical order, with one letter repeated.

Bookkeeper

This is the only common word that features three consecutive pairs of double letters. Now imagine the bookkeeper's assistant, a *subbookkeeper,* who boasts four consecutive pairs of double letters.

Now imagine a zoologist who helps maintain raccoon habitats. We'd call that zoologist a *raccoon nook keeper*—six consecutive sets of double letters! Now let's conjure up another zoologist who studies the liquid secreted by chickadee eggs. We'd call this scientist a *chickadee egg goo-ologist*—and into the world is born three consecutive sets of triple letters!

Camry

Look closely at the letters on a Camry automobile and you can make the kangaroo words MY CAR. A Camry is a Toyota. A TOYOTA is a palindrome, and each letter is itself a palindrome.

Connecticut

What begins with a union and ends with a separation? The answer is *Connecticut*, which can be charaded into the oxymoron *Connect I cut.*

Four

Four is the only number with a quantity of letters that matches its value.

Ghoti

George Bernard Shaw, who championed the cause of spelling reform, once announced that he had discovered a new way to spell the word *fish*. His fabrication was *ghoti*—*gh* as in enou*gh*, *o* as in w*o*men, and *ti* as in na*ti*on.

There are many other "fish" in the A-B-Sea.

Phusi: ph as in *physic, u* as in bu*s*y, *si* as in pen*si*on

*Ffess: o*ff, *pretty, issue*

Fish in the ABSea

Ghoti

Phusi

Ffess

Ughyce

Pfeechsi   Pphiapsh   Fuiseo

Ftaisch   Ueiscio

Dave Morice

*Ughyce: laugh, hymn, ocean
*Pfeechsi: Pfeiffer, been, fuchsia
*Pphiapsh: sapphire, marriage, pshaw
*Fuiseo: fat, guilt, nauseous
*Ftaisch: soften, villain, schwa
*Ueiscio: lieutenant (British pronunciation), forfeit, conscious.

Jason

The name Jason is composed of the first letters of five successive months—July, August, September, October, November. If James Jason were a DJ on FM/AM radio, the first letters of all 12 months would be represented sequentially:

J. JASON, DJ
FM/AM

John

The name John (or Jon) can be changed into six different women's names or nicknames simply by changing the vowel sound:

Jan	Jen
Jane	Joan
Jean	June

LLANFAIRPWLLGWYNGYNGYLLGOGERYCHWYRNDROBWLLLLANTYSILIOGOGOCH

This is the Welsh name of a village railway station in Alglesey, Gwynedd, Wales, cited in the *Guiness Book of World Records*. Translated, the name means "Saint Mary's Church in a hollow of white hazel, close to a whirlpool and Saint Tyslio's Church and near a red cave."

In addition to being one of the longest of place names, the fifty-six-letter cluster contains only one *e*.

Close kin is the Native American name for a lake near Webster, Massachusetts:

Chargoggagoggmanchauggogoggchaubunagungamaugg

which means "You fish on your side; I fish on my side; nobody fish in the middle." In its middle lurks the seven-letter palindrome—*ggogogg*. Fifteen of its 45 letters are *g*'s, and not one is an *i* or *e*.

MAINLAND

What are the longest words that we can cobble by stringing together a series of two-letter state postal abbreviations? "Stately words" of four letters abound, from *AKIN* (Alaska + Indiana) to *GAME* (Georgia + Maine) to *ORAL* (Oregon + Alabama) to *WINE* (Wisconsin + Nebraska). About twenty combinations of six letters can be found, from *ALMOND* (Alabama + Missouri + North Dakota) to *INCOME* (Indiana + Colorado + Maine) to *VANDAL* (Virginia + North Dakota + Alabama).

Eight-letter strings are rare as black pearls. The best example is *MAINLAND* (Massachusetts + Indiana + Louisiana + North Dakota).

Mississippi

In letter patterning, this is clearly the best of the state names. *Mississippi* contains just one vowel repeated four times, three sets of double letters, and only four different letters.

Overstuffed

Along with *overstudious* and *understudy*, *overstuffed* is stuffed with four touching letters of the alphabet in order.

Sequoia

The shortest word (seven letters) in which each major vowel appears once and only once. Eight-letter

Dave Morice

exhibits include *dialogue* and *equation*. *Sequoia* is further distinguished by a string of four consecutive vowels.

One up on *sequoia* is the word *queueing*, marked by five consecutive vowels. *Miaou* is listed in some dictionaries as an alternate spelling of *meow*. The past tense of *miaou* is *miaoued*—a seven-letter word that features an unbroken string of the five major vowels!

Sponged

Tied with *wronged, sponged* is the longest word (seven letters) with all its letters in reverse alphabetical order, with no letters repeated.

Spoonfeed

This is the longest word (nine letters) with all its letters in reverse alphabetical order, with some letters repeated.

Strengths

One of a number of nine-letter words of one syllable, and the longest containing but a single vowel. Among its strengths is the fact that it ends with five consecutive consonants.

Nine-letter, one-syllable words with more than one vowel include:

> *scratched   screeched   scrounged   squelched   stretched*

TWENTY-NINE

In capitalized form, TWENTY-NINE is formed from exactly 29 straight lines.

Typewriter

When we seek to find the longest word that can be typed on a single horizontal row of a standard typewriter keyboard, we naturally place our fingers on the top row of letters—

qwertyuiop—because five of the seven vowels reside there. From that single row we can type but a handful of ten-letter words, and one of them is *typewriter!*

United

With the interchange of neighboring letters, *united* becomes its opposite—*untied.*

Ushers

Has there ever been a word like *ushers?* Within *ushers* dwell almost all of humankind—five pronouns, with letters adjacent and in sequence: *he, her, hers, she,* and *us.*

After Word

Dave Morice

Each time the Greatest Show on Earth leaves a city, it tears itself down and piles itself onto railroad cars. Not so with the Circus of Words.

Nothing now to mark the spot
But a littered vacant lot.
Sawdust in a heap, and where
The center ring stood, grass worn bare.

But remains the alphabet,
Ready to leap and pirouette.
May the spangled letters soar
In your head forever more.

May all your days be circuses.

SOURCES

Responsible authors list the sources of their work. The most valuable source for this book has been *Word Ways*, (Morristown, NJ: 1968–2000).

All anagrams, palindromes, and other letter play are listed alphabetically followed by their earliest known sources. (Note: Many of the code names are for members of the National Puzzlers League.)

Letter Words

"The farmer leads no EZ life," H. C. Dodge, *Women's Home Companion*, July 1903.

Anagrams

ACT ON A BAR, Hoho; AH, AN ART GEM!, Guiden; AMEN STORIES, Lord Baltimore; CARE IS NOTED, DCVer; COME TRUST UP HERE, Enavlicm; DIRTY ROOM, T. H.; GOLDEN LAND, *Farmer's Almanac*; GRAND OLD EVILS, Johank; HE IN NET SPORT, AbStruse; HE'S LETTER POST MANGER, Tunste; HOT SUN, OR LIFE IN A CAR, Josefa Heifetz.

I'M A DOT IN PLACE, Achem; I'M A HACKER, SON, Atlantic; I'M TRADES EVENTS, DCVer; I PLAY ALL THE ABC, xspected; IS A LANE, AwlWrong; JOYFUL FOURTH, KingCarnival; LEAST IN SINS, NJineer; LOVE TO RUIN, Enavlicm; NO WIRE UNSENT, LeDare; PEN MATE IN LOVE, Hoodwink; RUN, PEST, Viking; RUNS A TREAT, WillieWildwater; SHALL YET COME MCS; VOICES RANT ON, SamWeller.

Palindromes

A DOG/PAGODA, Lubin; AHEM!/HA!, Stephen J. Chism; A MAN!/PANAMA!, ARE/ERA?, DEER/FREED, Leigh Mercer; DOC/COD, Peter Hilton; DRAW/UPWARD, Howard Bergerson; DUDE/DUD, Jim Hebert; ELK CACKLE, John Connett; EMIL/LIME, Chism; GATEMAN/NAME TAG, Mercer; GO HANG/HOG, John Agee; GOD, A RED NUGGET/DOG, Mercer.

I SAW DESERTS/WAS I, Bergerson; LID/DAFFODIL, John Pool; MADAM, I'M ADAM, Mercer; MARGE/TELEGRAM, Bergerson; MAY/YAM, Pool; NEVER/EVEN, Willard Espy; NIAGARA/AGAIN, Bergerson; NOW NED/WON, Mercer; NURSE/RUN!, Mercer; OH, WHO/OH WHO?, E. J. McIlvaine; PANDA/NAP, John Pool; POOR/DROOP, Bergerson.

RATS GNASH/STAR, Mercer; RATS LIVE/EVIL STAR, Bergerson; RISE/SIR, Bergerson; SIDES/IS, J. Linden; SO MANY DYNAMOS, Pool; SIT/OTIS, Dmitri Borgmann; STAR/DEMOCRATS, the Kuhns; STELLA WALLETS, Dmitri Borgmann; STRAW/WARTS, Mercer; TEN/NET, Mercer; TOO/HOOT, Morton Mitchell; WAS IT/CAT I SAW?, Marvin Terban.

Beheadings and Curtailments

PEARL/PEAR/PEA, Dave Morice.

A number of the beheadings appear in *Word Ways*, May 1990, and the curtailments in Ralph G. Beaman, *Word Ways*, February 1976.

Charade Words
SO, A POP ERA, Michael-Sean Lazarchuk.

Pangrams
"Mr. Jock, TV quiz Ph.D., bags few lynx" is generally attributed to Clement Wood.

Mirror Words
AHTAWAIH, Dave Morice, *Word Ways*, November 1996.

Mary Poems
e and *a* lipograms, A. Ross Eckler, *Word Ways*, August 1969; *e* univocalic, Paul Hellweg, *Word Ways*, August 1986; anagrams, James Rambo, *Word Ways*, February 1989; line palindromes, Peter Newby and Dave Morice, *Word Ways*, November 1990, and second verse, Richard Lederer.

Chace, Howard L. *Anguish Languish,* Englewood Cliffs, NJ: Prentice Hall, 1956.

INDEX OF TERMS

About the Author

Richard Lederer has actually been elected International Punster of the Year, the fastest punslinger in the world. He writes best-selling language books, including *Anguished English*, and is usage editor for the *Random Dictionary of the English Language, Third Edition, Unabridged.* Lederer's other book by Chicago Review Press is *Pun & Games*. He writes a column called "Looking at Language" and hosts a one-hour public radio show called "A Way with Words."

You can e-mail him at richard.lederer@pobox.com and visit his Web site at www.verbivore.com.

About the Illustrator

Dave Morice is an award-winning illustrator, writer, and poet. He holds an M.F.A. from the Iowa Writers' Workshop and has taught children's literature at the University. Morice is a distinguished letterer in his own right as the longtime columnist for *Word Ways* and the author of many books, including *Poetry Comics* and *The Dictionary of Wordplay*.